W9-BDY-418

BLIC LIBRARY DISTRICT OF COLUMBIA

Sampson

Sampson THE CHRISTMAS CAT

STORY AND PICTURES BY
CATHERINE STOCK

G. P. PUTNAM'S SONS
New York

Text and illustrations copyright © 1984 by Catherine Stock.
All rights reserved.
Published simultaneously in
Canada by General Publishing Co. Limited, Toronto.
Printed in the United States of America.
Library of Congress Cataloging in Publication Data
Stock, Catherine.
Sampson, the Christmas cat.
Summary: On Christmas morning a stray cat slips
into the house through an open window,
and the children decide to keep him,
hidden in an old basket under the stairs.
1. Children's stories, American. [1. Cats—Fiction.
2. Christmas—Fiction] I. Title
PZ7.S8635Sam 1984 [E] 84-9946
ISBN 0-399-21002-4
First impression.

LAR.
JUV.

For my special friend, Nora

3 1172 01578 3905

It was Christmas morning when Sampson arrived at 27 Christopher Street. He didn't come wrapped in satin ribbon and tissue paper like the other gifts. He slipped in through a slightly open kitchen window.

Sarah found him padding across the table toward the turkey. She shouted, and Sampson knocked over three jars of cranberry jelly.

Bill and Lizzie rushed into the kitchen.

"What's that cat doing in here?" said Lizzie.

"Catch him," shouted Bill.

Sampson wondered whether he had time to snatch a drumstick before leaping out the window.

Before he could decide, Sarah picked him up and held him tightly. "Let's keep him," she whispered.

"Where?" Lizzie wondered. "Mother doesn't like cats."

"We can hide him in a trunk in the cellar," Bill said.

Sampson squealed and wriggled desperately.

"Don't be silly," Lizzie said. "We can hide him in an old basket under the stairs."

"And give him some sardines to eat," said Sarah. Sampson snuggled up and purred.

Sampson didn't mind hiding under the stairs. He was warm and full of sardines and milk. He closed his eyes and dreamed of turkey leftovers.

Mother walked right by Sampson and didn't see him.

But she did see three empty sardine cans under the table.

"I was hungry," said Bill.

And she found the bottle of milk half empty in the refrigerator.

"I was thirsty," said Sarah.

A red cushion was missing from the couch in the living room.

"It had a hole, and I'm going to mend it," Lizzie said.

But the muddy pawprints on the clean kitchen tablecloth?

Luckily the doorbell rang before Mother saw them.

"Happy Christmas, everybody!" Uncle Fred and Aunt Sally had arrived for Christmas dinner. Behind them stood Susie and George, Nora and Carolyn.

And then there was Bert.

“I wonder what he’ll do this year,” whispered Sarah, remembering last Christmas when Bert filled the sugar bowl with salt,

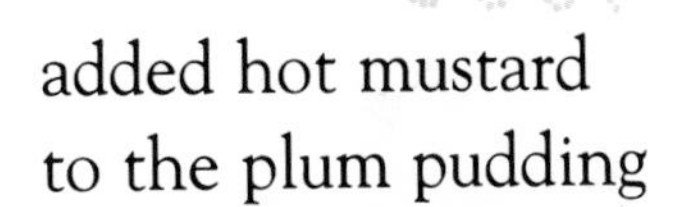

added hot mustard to the plum pudding

and banged his new drum after lunch, when everyone was dozing.

"Squee . . ."

This year it was a tickler. A long green feather that tickled ears and noses and eyes. Around the room went Bert. "*Squee!*"

Uncle Fred smiled (he didn't hear very well), and Aunt Sally sighed.

"Put that away, Bert," she said.

"*Squeeee!*" shrilled the tickler, louder than ever.

“*Meeoouuw!*”

Out of nowhere a large orange ball of fur flew through the air and landed on the tickler. And Bert.

Everyone stared at the fat cat sprawled across Bert in a tangled mess of green feathers, looking embarrassed.

How could I mistake a tickler for a mouse! Sampson was horrified.

He got up, unwound his whiskers, straightened out his tail, and walked toward the door with his head held high.

"Hooray for Sampson," Sarah cried.

"Hooray," said Lizzie and Bill.

"Mother, please can he stay?" Sarah begged.

Mother was laughing. "I'm not sure he wants to," she said.

Sampson paused. It was getting dark outside. He thought he saw some raindrops splatter against the window.

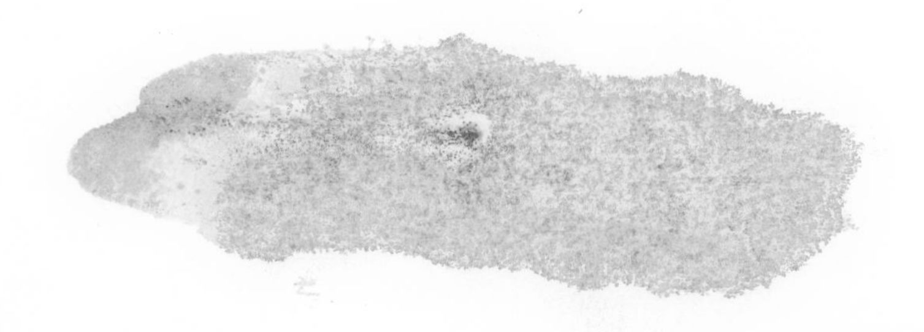

Sampson turned and padded toward the fire. He jumped into a chair and looked back at everyone. He would think it over. Then he yawned, prodded the cushion, and settled down to a little nap before dinner, while everyone opened their presents.